# Mrs. Peloki's Class Play

Story by Joanne Oppenheim
Pictures by Joyce Audy dos Santos

Dodd, Mead & Company
New York

I   2   3   4   5   6   7   8   9   10

Library of Congress Cataloging in Publication Data

Oppenheim, Joanne.
  Mrs. Peloki's class play.

  Summary: After a disastrous dress rehearsal, the second-grade play
is a great success but has an unexpected ending.
  |1. Plays—Fiction.  2. Schools—Fiction.  3. Humorous
stories|  I. Dos Santos, Joyce Audy, ill.   II. Title.
PZ7.O616Mr  1984        |E|        83-25457
ISBN 0-396-08178-9

To my daughter

☆

STEPHANIE

—J.O.

For Egils, my wonderful friend

—J.A.dS.

It was the day before our class play. We were on stage for our last rehearsal of *Cinderella*. We had been practicing for weeks and weeks. I was the star. I was Cinderella.

The scenery was painted and our costumes were made. Mrs. Peloki, our teacher, said, "All right, let's do our best. This is our dress rehearsal."

"I'm not wearing no dress!" Marlon said. He made that dumb joke every time someone said "dress rehearsal."

"Mrs. Peloki!" Danny yelled. "Billy stepped on my tail."

"I didn't see it," said Billy. He followed Danny onstage. They were funny-looking mice.

"Now listen to me!" Mrs. Peloki scolded. "We have no time for silliness. Not from the mice or the prince or anyone. I'm going out front so I can hear you. You're going to do the whole play straight through without stopping, no matter what. Remember, the show must go on."

So we started. And it went all right until the ugly stepsisters,
MariEllen and Angie, were dressing for the ball. MariEllen said,
"Cinderella, comb my hair," and then Angie yelled, "*I'm* supposed to
say that. She took my line again, Mrs. Peloki."

"Just keep going," Mrs. Peloki called from the back of the auditorium.
"Go ahead, Cinderella."

But I didn't know whose hair to comb first.

Then we got to the part where I say, "I wish I could go to the ball."
That's when the lights are supposed to flash, and the fairy godmother
is supposed to pop out of the fireplace.

Only James flashed the auditorium lights instead of the stage lights,
and Wendy, the fairy godmother, couldn't get out of the fireplace.

"I'm stuck! My wings are stuck!" she hollered.

"Forget the wings," Mrs. Peloki called. "Just keep going."

After the fairy godmother came unstuck, she told me to bring her a
pumpkin. But Eddie had his pumpkin box on backwards. His coach
side was showing.

"You dummy," the fairy godmother giggled.

"It's not funny," called Mrs. Peloki. "Turn around, Edward. And
Cinderella, louder please!"

My throat was getting sore from talking so loud.

Then in the ball scene we were supposed to dance, only there wasn't any music.

James came on stage with the tape recorder. "It's not my fault," he said. "The batteries must be dead."

It was the worst rehearsal we ever had.

"All right, boys and girls, quiet down." Mrs. Peloki sighed. "Now I don't want you to worry. Tomorrow will be fine."

"Not if that jerk steps on my tail," Danny grumbled.

"Accidents happen," said Mrs. Peloki. "There's an old saying in the theater. 'A bad dress rehearsal is good luck.' You'll see. Tomorrow will be perfect. Just be sure to get a good night's sleep."

But that night I kept dreaming about the play. It was a nightmare.

The fairy godmother was a wicked witch.

The pumpkin turned into a dragon instead of a coach.

One of the mice turned into a lion instead of a footman.

And when the fairy godmother waved her wand, my dress fell off.

"Just a bad dream, dear," my mom said.

"I don't feel good," I told her.

"Go back to sleep, Stephie. It's just butterflies."

The next day when I got to school, our room was noisy and I felt awful. Billy was chasing Danny and knocked him into Wendy.

"My wand!" screamed Wendy. "He broke my fairy godmother wand!"

"Mrs. Peloki," sobbed MariEllen. "Tell James to stop calling me ugly."

James shrugged. "But that's what she's supposed to be, an ugly stepsister."

"No one's calling *me* ugly," Angie bragged.

"Enough!" said Mrs. Peloki. "I want every one of you to go to your desk. I'll fix your wand, Wendy. And stop the crying, MariEllen. You are a beautiful ugly stepsister."

"Mrs. Peloki!" I needed to tell her I really didn't feel good.

But Mrs. Peloki said, "Please go to your seat, Cinderella. Now where is our prince charming? Has anyone seen Marlon?"

Eddie pointed to the closets.

Mrs. Peloki opened one closet door after another. "What's the
matter, Marlon? Come out, please."
"I'm not coming out like this."
"Marlon, what's wrong?"

"I'm not wearing no lipstick, and I don't see why you told my mom to make me wear tights."

"Oh, dear," said Mrs. Peloki. "A prince can't wear jeans and sneakers, Marlon. Now you look just like a storybook prince. That's what men wore in olden days."

It wasn't easy, but Mrs. Peloki finally managed to get Marlon to come out. "All right, boys and girls, it's almost ten o'clock. Time for us to line up."

"Now?" MariEllen giggled nervously. "I'm going to faint, I know it. When the curtain opens, I'm going to pass out."

"I'm so scared, I've got to go!" Wendy made a dash for the bathroom.

"Watch those wings," warned Mrs. Peloki.

"I feel awfully funny inside," I said.

"Just butterflies." Mrs. Peloki smiled at us. "You'll do fine. Remember, today is no different from any other day."

"Except the whole school will be watching," shouted Billy.

"And our mothers," said Angie.

"And fathers," added Kevin.

"Yes, and my grandma is bringing my little brother," said MariEllen.

"So what," said James, "my grandma is bringing her camera."

"This lipstick tastes yucky," Billy complained.

Mrs. Peloki laughed. "You're not supposed to eat it. Now, here's the fairy godmother and we're ready. Remember, I expect everyone to use big voices." She was looking at me.

"Okey-dokey, Mrs. Peloki," James started in. Then everyone was
saying it. "Okey-dokey, Mrs. Peloki. Okey-dokey, Mrs. Peloki."

"Sh-sh-sh!" Mrs. Peloki warned us as we went backstage.
Through the closed curtain we could hear the audience talking and
laughing. Danny and Billy peeked underneath.

"Boys," Mrs. Peloki whispered, "they'll see you."

"What a mob," said Billy.

"No talking," Mrs. Peloki scolded. "James? Where's James?" James was right behind her, but Mrs. Peloki was so jittery I guess she didn't notice.

The minute James stepped out between the curtains, the audience was silent.

"Parents, teachers, and friends," he began. "Thank you for coming to Cooke School. Our second grade is proud to present *Cinderella*. But first please stand to say the Pledge of Allegiance."

I wondered if James would remember to put his right hand on his heart. I could feel my own heart thumping as we pledged the flag, even though we couldn't see it. All of a sudden, I couldn't remember one word I was supposed to say. I started feeling kind of itchy all over.

  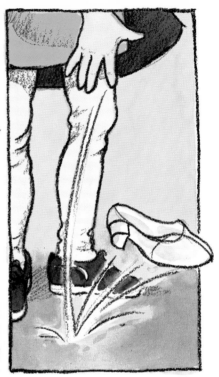

Then, when the curtain opened, a little voice in the audience yelled,
"Mommy, look. There's MariEllen. Hi, MariEllen!"

I would have died if my little brother had said that, but MariEllen
just waved. From then on everything worked. Well, practically
everything.

One of Billy's mouse ears fell off, but he just picked it up and carried
it around.

James lost count on the chimes and rang thirteen instead of twelve
o'clock midnight.

And in the last scene, the prince dropped the glass slipper, but it
didn't break, because it was really plastic.

Finally we got to the end, where the prince is supposed to kiss me. I
knew Marlon wouldn't, so I kissed him. Everyone was clapping for us
and snapping our pictures. Mrs. Peloki said she was very proud of us,
and she loved the flowers we gave her.

After all that worrying, I was sorry it was over. My throat was sore, but
I kept wishing we could do the whole play again…until Billy hollered,
"Steph! Your face! You look weird!"
And Wendy screamed, "Oh, no! Look at Cinderella!"
"What's wrong with that girl?" Marlon's mother asked.
"Don't touch me!" yelled James.

"Oh, Stephie!" My mom felt my head. "She's burning hot."

"Poor child," sighed Mrs. Peloki.

"They'll all have it now." Danny's mother put her arms around him.

"Oh, man, she never should have kissed me," Marlon said with disgust.

And I guess he was right. My butterflies were gone, but I had something else.

I was the first Cinderella to end up with the chicken pox instead of
a prince.